I0893127

INVESTIGATING PLASTIC POLLUTION

LAURA PERDEW

Wonder Books
An Imprint of The Child's World®
childsworld.com

The Child's World
childsworld.com

Published by The Child's World®
800-599-READ • www.childsworld.com

Copyright © 2023 by The Child's World®
All rights reserved. No part of this book may be reproduced or utilized in any form or by any means without written permission from the publisher.

Photography Credits
Photographs ©: Romolo Tavani/Shutterstock Images, cover, 2; Chase Dekker/Shutterstock Images, 5; Claude Huot/Shutterstock Images, 6; Kev Gregory/Shutterstock Images, 8; Mohamed Abdulraheem/Shutterstock Images, 9; Larina Marina/Shutterstock Images, 11; Shutterstock Images, 13, 14, 16 (beach), 16 (animals), 16 (road), 16 (buildings), 16 (boats), 19, 29; Lebedeva Alena/Shutterstock Images, 16 (plastic waste); iStockphoto, 20; Frans Blok/Shutterstock Images, 23; Milenova Elena/Shutterstock Images, 25; Igisheva Maria/Shutterstock Images, 27; Aleksey Boyko/Shutterstock Images, 31

ISBN Information
9781503858053 (Reinforced Library Binding)
9781503860124 (Portable Document Format)
9781503861480 (Online Multi-user eBook)
9781503862845 (Electronic Publication)

LCCN 2021952371

Printed in the United States of America

ABOUT THE AUTHOR

Laura Perdew is a mom, writing consultant, and author of more than 40 books for children. She lives and plays in Boulder, Colorado.

Sea animals such as turtles are affected by plastic pollution.

TABLE OF CONTENTS

CHAPTER ONE

PLASTIC POLLUTION

On a small boat out on the ocean near California, a family spotted a giant humpback whale. But the whale was not moving. They watched the whale for a few minutes. At last, it exhaled. Water spouted into the air.

Still, something seemed wrong. They used binoculars to get a closer look. The family saw that the whale was tangled in discarded plastic fishing nets. The whale was exhausted. Her fins were pinned against her body by the nets. Her tail had so much netting around it that she could not even hold herself up. The family knew that the whale would die without help.

The family quickly radioed for help. They told first responders about the whale.

Human pollution can have a large impact on wildlife. People can take steps to avoid plastic pollution.

Humpback whales jump from the water when they want to communicate with other whales.

Soon, help was on the way. Trained rescuers grabbed the plastic fishing nets that trapped the whale. Then they used a special cutting tool to cut the plastic. Over hours, they cut the netting bit by bit.

Somehow the whale knew that the people were helping her, not hurting her. She did not fight them. She did not try to hurt them. The rescuers took turns cutting the fishing net.

A SHORT HISTORY OF PLASTIC

Around 3,500 years ago, the Olmec people of present-day Mexico used sap from gum trees to make rubber balls. In the 1800s, scientists began experimenting with other plant materials to make plastic. In the early 1900s, scientists created the first plastic made only with chemicals. They continued to make new types of plastics for different uses. During World War II (1939–1945), plastic was used for helmets, raincoats, nylon parachutes, and more. After the war, plastic factories began making more and more products for everyday people.

The rescuers were exhausted, too. But they kept cutting. Finally, the giant whale was free. The rescuers pulled the net aboard their boat. They did not want other animals to get tangled in it. The whale swam a short distance away and leaped from the water. Everyone cheered.

Fishing nets are one of the millions of products made from plastic. Today, plastic is made from chemicals in oil and natural gas. It is a material that is both light and strong.

Plastic can also be molded into many different shapes. It can be thick or thin. And it can be clear or colored.

Plastic can be used to make almost anything. And because of its strength and usefulness, plastic can be found just about everywhere. It is used in homes, schools, offices, cars, electronics, and more. Unfortunately, plastic takes hundreds of years to break down. And it is difficult to recycle. A lot of it ends up in the ocean. This harms marine life and marine **ecosystems**. Today, many people are working together to reduce plastic pollution.

Fishing nets that are lost or abandoned are very dangerous to sea animals. Turtles and seals can get trapped in fishing nets. They cannot get out unless someone helps them.

CHAPTER TWO

PLANET PLASTIC

Plastic is an incredible material. It is used to make millions of different products. Many important products are made of plastic. This includes **prosthetics**, parts for electronics, and safety gear for sports.

Most trash that is thrown away ends up in landfills. Landfills are places where trash is stored and buried.

However, half of the products made from plastic are single-use items. Plastic bags, straws, and water and soda bottles are examples of items used only once and then thrown away.

All this plastic has led to a plastic pollution problem. Each stage of a plastic's life cycle is harmful to the environment. Removing and transporting the oil and gas to create plastic releases **greenhouse gases**. So does making the actual plastic at a factory. In many places, discarded plastic is burned. The burning releases greenhouse gases, too. Many plastics end up in the environment. Sunlight and heat cause the plastic to release even more greenhouse gases. All of this contributes to **global warming**.

Many towns and cities around the world are trying to recycle plastic. But plastic is hard to recycle. It is also an expensive process that releases greenhouse gases.

Plastic water bottles can take up to 500 years to decompose.

Additionally, less than 10 percent of all plastics are actually recycled.

Plastic that is not recycled, burned, or reused tends to end up in landfills and waterways. Unlike food waste or paper waste, plastic does not decompose. That means every bit of plastic ever made is still on the planet.

Over hundreds of years, plastic breaks down. But it does not go away completely.

Pieces of plastic just get smaller and smaller. Some of these pieces can be .2 inches (5 mm) or smaller. These pieces are called microplastics.

Microplastics are found in every place on Earth. They have been discovered in deep-sea trenches and on high mountaintops. They are in the soil and water. Microplastics have been found in remote deserts and in the ice of Arctic regions. Scientists have even found microplastics in air and rain.

SOURCES OF MICROPLASTICS

Many microplastics come from bigger items that break down after they are thrown away. Microplastics also come from tires, carpeting, and furniture that are still being used. Normal wear of these items sheds tiny microplastic fibers. Even most clothing is made from man-made materials that include plastic. Cozy fleece jackets are made of polyester, a type of plastic. When clothing is washed, small fibers come off. Eventually, these microplastics make their way into waterways.

Microplastics can be found in the ocean and in the sand.

Microplastics are also in some of the drinking water and foods people eat. That means humans breathe in, drink, and eat microplastics. The potential harm to humans is still being investigated. Most research is focused on the harm to marine life, where the plastic pollution problem is at its worst.

CHAPTER THREE

PLASTIC IN THE OCEAN

The biggest plastic pollution problem is in the ocean. Every year, at least 8 million tons (7.3 million metric tons) of plastic end up in the world's oceans. That is like one truckload of plastic dumped in the ocean every minute of every day. Yet most plastic is not dumped in the ocean on purpose. Sometimes, during bad weather, cargo ships lose containers in the water. Other times, fishing nets and lines are lost or abandoned.

Some areas of water are packed with garbage.

However, 80 percent of the plastic pollution in the ocean starts on land. Any plastic that is not properly discarded becomes litter. When it rains, litter is washed into storm drains, ditches, streams, and other waterways. Those waterways dump the waste into larger rivers. The waste is then carried out to the ocean, contributing to the marine pollution problem.

Plastic marine **debris** is all over the ocean. It is on the water's surface and the deep seafloor. There is marine debris along coasts and in the open ocean. There are also rotating currents in the open ocean. These giant whirlpools collect the marine debris in different areas. These areas are called garbage patches. There are five garbage patches on Earth. The debris in each of the garbage patches is mostly plastic.

The largest garbage patch is called the Great Pacific Garbage Patch. It is in the Pacific Ocean between Hawaii and California.

PLASTIC WASTE AND THE OCEAN

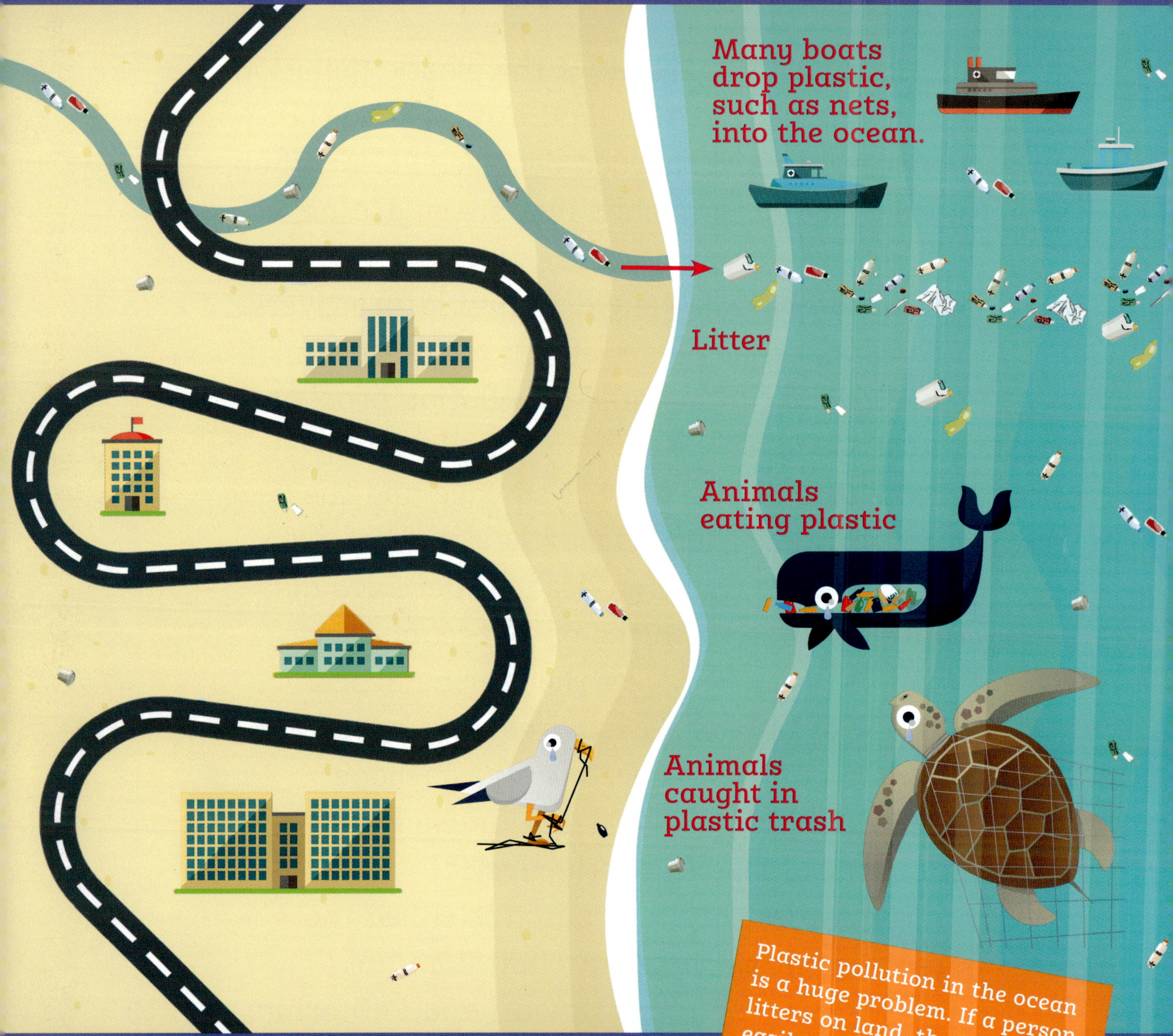

Plastic pollution in the ocean is a huge problem. If a person litters on land, the trash can easily end up in the ocean. This can then affect birds and animals living in the ocean.

It covers an area twice the size of Texas. Unlike the Great Pacific Garbage Patch, not all garbage patches are visible. They do not form an island or a raft of trash. Instead, the debris is scattered across the surface and down to the seafloor. There may be some large pieces of debris. But garbage patches are mostly made up of microplastics.

All the plastic in the ocean affects marine life. Many species eat microplastics. Even the smallest animals in the ecosystem eat microplastics. When larger animals eat smaller animals, they are also eating the microplastics and bad chemicals they contain. The plastic may not harm the animals right away. But it is toxic, which means it is poisonous. These toxins can slowly affect an animal's health, movement, reproduction, and survival skills.

Larger pieces of plastic are also a problem for marine life. Sometimes animals eat plastic, thinking it is food. A floating plastic bag in the ocean can look like a jellyfish to a sea turtle. Large seabirds, like albatrosses, skim the surface of the ocean for food. As they go, they pick up plastic. In these cases, the animals' stomachs are full, but not with food and nutrition. Instead, the birds' stomachs are filled with plastic. This can lead to death. In addition, many marine animals get tangled in plastic pollution. This often injures the animals. Others starve because they cannot move when they need to hunt for food.

Marine habitats are affected by plastic pollution, too. Coral reefs are important ecosystems in the ocean. Approximately 25 percent of marine species depend on coral reefs. But they are also fragile. Plastic pollution can break, smother, and damage these reefs. It can keep corals from growing.

It can even kill them. Along the coasts, ocean currents bring plastic pollution back to land. As a result, many shorelines are filled with plastic trash. All that plastic pollution hurts the coastal ecosystem. It also harms animals living there.

Plastic bags that get stuck in coral reefs can block the sunlight. This can damage the coral reefs, because they need sunlight to survive.

One way people can help reduce pollution is by doing beach cleanups.

CHAPTER FOUR

REDUCING PLASTIC POLLUTION

Plastic pollution affects the environment. It affects animal and human health. However, people are working to fix the problem.

Many communities and organizations hold cleanup events. Volunteers wear rubber gloves and carry trash bags. They spend the day picking up trash. This is especially important along the coast. Anything volunteers pick up does not end up back in the ocean.

Cleanups are important all year round. There is an International Coastal Cleanup Day every September. During this event, more than one million people around the world volunteer. They team up to collect debris on beaches.

In 2018, volunteers from 122 countries picked up more than 23 million pounds (10 million kg) of trash. Most of it was plastic.

Cleaning up the world's oceans is a harder challenge. But many people and organizations are developing technology to help with this problem. There are systems that help stop trash at the mouths of rivers. If it is stopped there, it would not reach the ocean. For example, the Waterfront Partnership of Baltimore developed trash wheels. Each trash wheel has long floating arms. These arms funnel debris to a conveyor belt. The conveyor belt is powered by the water current and the sun. It moves the trash up and into a dumpster. This system has collected millions of pounds of trash. Another organization, the Ocean Cleanup, is making a larger, different kind of system. They are working on pulling trash from ocean garbage patches.

The Ocean Cleanup organization is working to clean polluted oceans and rivers.

Scientists are also developing biodegradable plastic. These plastics are made to decompose when thrown away. They are made from plants, fungi, and other biodegradable materials instead of **fossil fuels** such as oil. In Mexico, avocado pits are being used to make plastic, too.

Other people are going one step further. In 2017, researchers discovered that a wax worm can chemically break down plastic. Also, some scientists found that bacteria and fungi could be used to work on the plastic problem. The bacteria and fungi eat and transform plastic into nontoxic materials. In 2018, scientists created an **enzyme** that could break down plastic in a couple days.

THINK ABOUT THE MATH

It may not seem like carrying a reusable water bottle to school or sports practice is helping the plastic pollution problem. But think about the math. If there are 180 school days in a year, that means 180 fewer single-use plastic water bottles are used. If a whole class of 25 students does that for the school year, that keeps 2,000 bottles from being used and discarded. What would happen if the whole school began using reusable water bottles? How many single-use plastic bottles would be avoided if a sports team did that for an entire season?

A scientist in India developed a spoon that can be eaten. Bakey's Edible Cutlery was created in 2011. Their products are alternatives to plastic utensils. These edible utensils are made with rice, millet, and wheat. There are also many flavors. Now, other companies are making edible utensils, too.

Another solution to plastic pollution is using less plastic. Everyone can help. People can start by saying "no" to single-use plastic. That can mean not using plastic straws.

Along with edible utensils, people have made edible cups.

Reducing plastic pollution can look like taking reusable bags to the store. When ordering takeout, people can use knives, forks, and spoons from home. They can also carry a reusable water bottle. Also, people can buy food in bulk to reduce packaging waste.

Many places around the world have banned single-use plastic. In 2007, San Francisco, California, was the first U.S. city to ban plastic grocery bags. The state of California banned them in 2014. Since then, dozens of cities and states have put a similar ban in place. Other bans have followed. There are bans on plastic straws, utensils, and foam containers. In Europe, a ban on many single-use plastics went into effect in 2021. In addition, Europe set a goal that by 2030, all plastic packaging must be recyclable.

Another way to help slow and stop plastic pollution is to raise awareness.

Instead of using plastic items, people can use reusable bags, metal straws, and reusable drink containers.

Some communities do this by hosting cleanup events. Others make recycling containers readily available. Some artists also use plastic waste to create sculptures and other pieces of art. The artwork brings attention to the plastic pollution problem. The more people know about the harmful effects of plastic and how to reduce its use, the more likely they are to be part of the plastic pollution solution.

FAST FACTS

- Plastic is made from chemicals found in oil and natural gas.
- Plastic is strong, long-lasting, and lightweight. It is easily molded into different shapes.
- Plastic does not ever decompose. It just breaks down into smaller and smaller bits called microplastics.
- Microplastics are found everywhere on Earth. They are in remote areas, as well as in the air and rain.
- Making and throwing away plastic contributes to global warming.
- The plastic pollution problem impacts the world's oceans the most. It harms marine wildlife and ecosystems.
- Scientists are developing biodegradable plastics and other alternatives to plastics made from oil and gas.
- New campaigns are raising awareness of the negative impact of plastic. They are trying to ban single-use plastics to reduce plastic pollution.

MAKE BIODEGRADABLE PLASTIC

MATERIALS

- ☐ 4 tablespoons of water
- ☐ 1 tablespoon of cornstarch
- ☐ 1 teaspoon of vinegar
- ☐ 1 teaspoon of glycerin
- ☐ Cooking pot
- ☐ Whisk
- ☐ Wooden spoon
- ☐ Cookie sheet

DIRECTIONS

1. Combine 4 tablespoons of water, 1 tablespoon of cornstarch, and 1 teaspoon of vinegar in a cooking pot. Add 1 teaspoon of glycerin. Whisk together on medium heat.
2. Stir constantly. When the mixture thickens, use a wooden spoon to continue stirring.
3. After about ten minutes, the mixture will be sticky and glassy. Carefully remove it from the heat. Spread the mixture in a thin layer on the cookie sheet.
4. Set aside to dry for one day. Then peel it off. You have created your own biodegradable plastic!

GLOSSARY

debris (duh-BREE) Debris is a piece of waste left scattered around. Most marine debris is plastic.

ecosystems (EE-koh-siss-tuhms) Ecosystems are made up of living things and their environments. Marine ecosystems are hurt by plastic pollution.

enzyme (EN-zime) An enzyme is a substance made by an organism that causes chemical reactions. Scientists have found an enzyme that eats plastic.

fossil fuels (FOSS-uhl FYOO-uhls) Coal, oil, and natural gas are examples of fossil fuels. Burning fossil fuels creates pollution.

global warming (GLOHB-uhl WARM-ing) Global warming is the rise in the temperature of Earth's atmosphere. The release of greenhouses gases contributes to global warming.

greenhouse gases (GREEN-howss GAS-ez) Greenhouse gases are gases that trap heat in Earth's atmosphere. Earth's temperature is rising because there are too many greenhouse gases.

prosthetics (prahs-THET-iks) Prosthetics are artificial body parts made to replace parts that are missing. Many prosthetics replace limbs such as legs, helping people walk again.

WAYS YOU CAN HELP

- Do not use single-use plastics. This includes plastic water bottles, straws, utensils, and bags.
- Participate in a cleanup event to help keep plastic pollution from entering waterways.
- Recycle plastic items whenever possible.
- Help raise awareness by spreading the word about the plastic pollution problem and how individuals can help.

FIND OUT MORE

In the Library

Beer, Julie. *Kids vs. Plastic*. Washington, DC: National Geographic, 2020.

Blom, Kirsti. *Plastic Sea: A Bird's-Eye View*. Apex, NC: Cornell Lab, 2020.

French, Jess. *What a Waste*. New York, NY: DK Publishing, 2019.

On the Web

Visit our website for links about investigating plastic pollution: **childsworld.com/links**

Note to Parents, Teachers, and Librarians: We routinely verify our Web links to make sure they are safe and active sites. So encourage your readers to check them out!

INDEX